The first Thanksgiving Ethan could remember, when he was just a little, little boy, and certainly not big enough and old enough to play in the annual family Turkey Bowl, the weather was so frigid they called the Turkey Bowl the Ice Bowl.

Aunt Yvonne wore so many layers she could barely lift her arms and legs, while Cousin Corey's hair and beard grew frozen stalactites!

Ethan; his best friend, Alex; and all the kids from the block shivered and shouted from the first snap to the final score.

Another Thanksgiving, when Ethan was still just a little boy, and certainly not big enough and old enough to play in the family Turkey Bowl, the weather was so rainy and wet they called the Turkey Bowl the Mud Bowl.

Aunt Amy slid ten yards for one touchdown, while Cousin Chris splashed twenty more for another!

Ethan, Alex, and all the kids from the block chuckled and cheered during every last mud-splattered play.

And last Thanksgiving, when Ethan still wasn't quite big enough and old enough to play in the Turkey Bowl, the weather was so foggy and gray they called the Turkey Bowl the Fog Bowl.

On one play, Uncle Zack couldn't figure out which direction to run, while on another play Cousin Ryan ran right into the goalpost!

Ethan, Alex, and all the kids from the block squealed and squinted all game long . . . even on the plays they could only hear.

But this year, when those first familiar scents of mashed potatoes, candied yams, and macaroni and cheese wafted up the stairs and woke Ethan, he realized the Turkey Bowl was a whole new ball game.

For the first time, Ethan, Alex, and all the kids from the block were finally big enough and old enough to play.

"It's here! It's here!" he declared, slipping into his favorite football jersey and pants.

"See ya, sidelines! It's Ethan time!"

Bursting from his bedroom, Ethan scampered down the stairs and stormed into the kitchen. "Are you ready for some football?"

All the wonderful holiday sights welcomed his arrival: the golden turkey and glazed ham waiting their turns for the oven; the bubbling butternut squash soup simmering on the stove; the heaps of corn-bread stuffing lining the counter; and of course Mom, Dad, and Grandpa preparing pie after pie after pie: key lime, pumpkin, and pecan—one for each family on the block.

But the most important holiday ingredient was nowhere to be seen.

"Hey, where is everybody?" Ethan asked.

"I'm afraid Thanksgiving may be a little different this year," Mom said, shaking her head.

"Because of the snow, many of the roads are closed," added Dad. "And the open ones are far too dangerous."

Ethan was so disappointed he couldn't even speak.

Ethan opened the front door and stepped outside. Through snowflakes the size of golf balls, he gazed at the field at the end of the street.

"How can we have Thanksgiving without everyone?" He pulled off his helmet. "How can we play the Turkey Bowl?"

Ethan headed next door and broke the awful news to his best friend. Then Ethan and Alex trudged from house to house to house, spreading the word to all the kids from the block:

"The year we're finally able to play, look what happens," Alex said, slapping his sides. "No Turkey Bowl."

Ethan, Alex, and all the kids from the block sat atop the bleachers and stared gloomily at the empty, snow-covered schoolyard.

Suddenly, *the* idea hit Ethan harder than any quarterback sack or open-field tackle.

"Time out!" he shouted, leaping off the bleachers. "We can have our *own* Turkey Bowl. Just because my relatives aren't here, doesn't mean *we* can't play."

"We can call it Turkey Bowl Too!" Alex jumped down beside him.

Ethan, Alex, and all the kids from the block charged from those sidelines onto the frozen tundra, and seconds later . . .

Ethan plowed through a pile for the game's first touchdown.

Alex darted through a drift for the game's first interception.

And on one white, wacky play, the fumbled football disappeared beneath a mountain of bodies and snow!

All afternoon Ethan, Alex, and all the kids from the block dove for passes and lunged for tackles.

Finally, on the last play of the Turkey Bowl, Alex dropped back for a pass and threw a bomb. Ethan raced down the sidelines. Deep in the end zone, he soared high above a defender . . .

"Touchdown! Touchdown!"

Ethan could hardly believe his ears and eyes. Not only had the ball landed in his hands, but Aunt Amy, Cousin Chris, and everyone else was there to see it too!

"Everyone made it!" Ethan exclaimed at the family feast.

"Of course we made it," his relatives replied. "We could never miss Thanksgiving and Turkey Bowl Too!"